MEXICO

CABO SAN LUCAS INT'L AIRPORT

notes from a spinning planet

MEXICO

OTHER BOOKS FOR TEENS BY MELODY CARLSON

Notes from a Spinning Planet series
Diary of a Teenage Girl series
TrueColors series
Degrees of Betrayal series
Degrees of Guilt series
Letters from God for Teens
Piercing Proverbs

MEXICO

notes from a spinning planet

MEXICO

a novel

Melody Carlson

WATERBROOK
PRESS

NOTES FROM A SPINNING PLANET—MEXICO
PUBLISHED BY WATERBROOK PRESS
12265 Oracle Boulevard, Suite 200
Colorado Springs, Colorado 80921
A division of Random House Inc.

The characters and events in this book are fictional, and any resemblance to actual persons or events is coincidental.

ISBN: 978-1-4000-7146-3

Library of Congress Cataloging-in-Publication Data
Carlson, Melody.
    Notes from a spinning planet — Mexico / Melody Carlson. — 1st ed.
        p. cm.
    Summary: When Maddie joins her journalist aunt on vacation in Mexico, she finds a rival for Ryan's affection, a friend who has a drinking problem, and most important, a new trust in God.
    ISBN 978-1-4000-7146-3
    [1. Christian life—Fiction. 2. Mexico—Fiction. 3. Alcoholism—Fiction. 4. Inter-personal relations—Fiction. 5. Aunts—Fiction.] I. Title.
    PZ7.C216637 Nov 2007
    [Fic]—dc22

                                                    2007012421

Printed in the United States of America
2007—First Edition

10 9 8 7 6 5 4 3 2 1

ONE

The past few months have been seriously depressing. At first I thought it was the letdown of normal life after such an awesome summer traveling to exotic and exciting locales with my aunt. Then I blamed my mood on the weather, which has been dreary and gray and unusually chilly. Then I thought it was probably the fact that I've been stuck on the farm again, attending community college for fall semester, since I don't get to transfer to the University of Washington until January.

Of course, it didn't help matters that Lydia, my friend from Papua New Guinea, had to delay coming here until winter semester as well. So I've just been biting the bullet and telling myself this is simply a temporary delay. I even think I should enjoy this. Who knows? It could be the last time I live at home with my parents. I actually thought they might appreciate having me around, but suddenly I'm thinking they might be glad to see me go. I mean, it seems like they sort of enjoyed my absence this past summer, once my mom got over her overprotective paranoia, and now I realize it'll be the first time in about twenty-four years they won't have kids living under their roof. And I suppose they could be ready for a little empty-nest syndrome about now.

Consequently, when Aunt Sid called and asked if I could go to Mexico with her during winter break, I literally jumped and yelled, "*¡Olé!*" My mom was a little bummed that Sid booked our flights out of Seattle on the day after Christmas, but I am totally thrilled to get out of town.

Dad and I leave for the airport before the sun's even up, making pretty good time—until we get close to the city, that is, and heavy shopper traffic is backed up into next Tuesday. I try not to freak, but I feel fairly certain I could miss my flight. Finally we're at Sea-Tac, and I beg him to drop me at the terminal, convincing him that I'll be just fine. I even hold up my cell phone as proof.

"Look, as soon as I'm with Aunt Sid, I'll just call you, okay? That way you don't have to park, and hopefully I won't miss the plane."

He seems relieved. "Sounds good, Maddie." Then he kisses me good-bye and tells me to be careful. I lug my stuff up to the ticket counter and quickly check in with the electronic ticket Sid e-mailed me last week. Simple as can be. Or so I think as I jog toward the security gates, getting my boarding pass and photo ID ready. And then it hits me. I look back toward the ticketing area and realize it's too late. If I'm going to make this flight, I better just keep going.

I get through security without a hitch, although the woman behind me sets off all the alarms and ends up being searched. I grab my backpack and start running for the departure gate that's written on my ticket. When I get there, I'm out of breath, but there is Sid, standing by the counter and waving at me.

"Hurry, Maddie," she yells, like I haven't already been running my legs off.

"Sorry," I say breathlessly. "Traffic."

"That's all you're bringing?" she asks as we hand the gate agent our boarding passes. "I mean, I told you to pack light, but that's incredibly light."

I sheepishly smile as I sling my backpack over my shoulder. "I didn't even realize what I did until I was at the security check," I explain. "I was in such a hurry."

"You checked your bag?"

I nod as we go down the Jetway that leads to the plane. "I'm sorry, Sid. The guy just grabbed it from me. And he even offered to take it over to the scanner for me so I could take off to meet you."

She forces a smile. "Wow, I just hope it gets there okay. They've already loaded the flight."

"I thought about going back to see if I could get it," I say as we wait for the last stragglers ahead of us to get onto the plane. "But it was so late."

"Don't worry," she says. "Maybe it's for the best. A big bag might've slowed you down in security, and we really could've missed our flight. We'll sort it out in Cabo."

Then we're on the plane. Just like that. But to my stunned surprise, instead of heading toward the coach section as usual, Sid stops in first class, nodding to a pair of seats that look extremely roomy and comfy. I think she must be kidding.

"I decided to upgrade us," she explains as the flight attendant politely takes our coats and carry-on bags. "My frequent-flier miles were about to expire, and while I was waiting for you to get here, I found out they still had first-class seats available."

"Cool," I say as I sit down and rub my hand over the smooth leather chair. "Wow, I feel like I'm famous." Then I glance around to see if there's anyone recognizable up here. I think I see a couple of guys who play for the Seahawks. I ask Sid, and she nods in confirmation. Then she whispers that the guy directly to my right is one of Seattle's richest computer moguls, but the woman sitting with him is not his wife. The pretty blonde looks young enough to be his daughter, but I'm guessing by the way he's treating her that she's not.

"Did you guys have a good Christmas?" Sid asks as she thumbs through a *Forbes* magazine.

"It was okay. It was kind of hard not having Jake home. But I suppose it helped that Aunt Betsy and her family came."

"How's your mom's sister doing anyway? I haven't seen her in years."

I sort of laugh, remembering how glad I was to get away from Aunt Betsy's hyperactive five-year-old twins. "I think she's still pretty frazzled. Tyler and Taylor are a handful. Mom thinks that just because Betsy waited so long to have them, she spoils them rotten. Mom doesn't say this to her face, of course. But the decibel level at our house was about ten times the norm. Dad was so glad he had to drive me to Seattle today—just for the peace and quiet."

Sid grins. "Guess I won't beat myself up too badly now for not coming to your house for Christmas."

"So Ian didn't make it out after all?" I ask a bit hesitantly. The last I heard, it didn't look good. Sid was really hoping he'd be able to come from Ireland for Christmas. I'm not sure how serious they are, but I suspect she was pretty disappointed.

"It was just too busy at the restaurant," she explains. "It sounds like Christmastime is becoming a hot tourist season, and Ian didn't want to make extra work for his employees by taking off."

"That was thoughtful."

She nods and sets the magazine aside. "Ian is a thoughtful guy. He actually suggested that I should come to Ireland for the holidays."

"Oh, why didn't you?" I ask.

She frowns slightly. "Well, I'd already booked this trip. It seemed like that'd be cutting it pretty close. Not to mention I'd have some serious jet lag."

"Oh." Now I feel a little bit guilty, like if it wasn't for me, maybe she would've blown off this Mexico trip in favor of Ireland. Still, there's nothing I can do about that now.

"Besides," she laughs, "sunny Mexico or chilly, wet Ireland in the wintertime? Hmm. Which would you choose?"

"Mexico wins, hands down." I nod eagerly. "So did you and Ryan have a good Christmas anyway?" Based on the e-mails that my friend Ryan and I have been exchanging lately, I know he pretty much hung with Sid during the holidays, although I'm not sure what they did. Still, their being together is a relief to me. This is Ryan's first Christmas since his mom died, and Sid, his godmother, is probably the next best thing. I considered inviting Ryan to come stay with us at the farm, but then Aunt Betsy and her family decided to visit.

"Yes, Ryan and I stayed with Vicki and her family."

"Is Vicki your friend from college?" I ask.

"Right. She and Ryan's mom and I were very close. Anyway, Vicki and Ed, her husband, have this gorgeous place on Fox Island. And

Vicki, as usual, went all out for Christmas—the tree, the food, everything was just perfect. All their kids were home, and I think Ryan really had a good time with the young people. Vicki and Ed really know how to make folks feel at home."

"And it's their condo we're going to stay in?" I ask.

"Actually, it's a time-share. Ed and Vicki bought it last year, but they haven't even been down there yet. Her parents talked her into getting it. I guess it was a pretty good deal, and knowing Vicki, it's probably very nice. They'll be going to check it out at the end of January."

"Just being down there with the sun and the beach sounds awesome to me," I say as I lean back into the seat and sigh. "Thanks so much for inviting me!"

"Hey, you're turning out to be my favorite traveling companion, Maddie. And after all we went through in Papua New Guinea, I figured you deserve a nice vacation."

"Hey, I loved New Guinea," I remind her.

She nods. "I know, but it was a little rustic."

"That's just part of its charm."

"Well, my article about the AIDS crisis there was well received. And I did a second one about traveling to Papua New Guinea as a tourist. You know, what to see and what not to do. It comes out next month."

"Did you mention how people can repurchase their stolen passports at the airport?" I ask.

She laughs. "I did indeed."

"Good thing that didn't happen to us," I say. "We were in such a